The Bodigulpa

When Jenny Nimmo left school she became a working student in a repertory company. She remained in the theatre for five years and then went to Italy to teach English. On her return to Britain, she joined the BBC where she eventually became a director/editor on the children's television programme, *Jackanory*. She now lives in Wales with her artist husband and, occasionally, her three grown-up children.

'Chilling and innovative . . . a deliciously scary story' *Guardian*

Shock Shop is a superb collection of short, illustrated, scary books for younger readers by some of today's most acclaimed writers for children.

SHOCK SHOP

The Bodigulpa

Jenny Nimmo

Illustrated by David Roberts

MACMILLAN CHILDREN'S BOOKS

First published 2001 by Macmillan Children's Books

This edition published 2002 by Macmillan Children's Books
a division of Macmillan Publishers Limited
20 New Wharf Road, London N1 9RR
Basingstoke and Oxford
www.panmacmillan.com

Associated companies throughout the world

ISBN 0 330 39750 8

1 3 5 7 9 8 6 4 2

A CIP catalogue record for this book is available from
the British Library.

Typeset by Intype London Ltd
Printed and bound in Great Britain by Mackays of Chatham plc, Kent

Contents

At the bottom of the Lloyds' garden there was once a greenhouse. Not any longer. They knocked it down. And a good thing too. Something almost too gruesome to imagine happened in that greenhouse . . .

Chapter 1
What Happened to Granny Green?

Mr and Mrs Lloyd were very much your indoor type of people. They read newspapers, watched TV, ate, cooked, listened to their favourite music and sometimes helped their son, Daniel, with his homework. They never bothered about the garden. That's to say, they didn't actually do anything with it.

Occasionally, Mrs Lloyd would put Daniel's baby sister in the garden but only in her pram. She was well into the crawling stage and Mrs Lloyd didn't want her wriggling through the mud and shoving snails into her mouth. Baby Molly would soon get bored and start to scream.

Daniel didn't much like baby Molly. In his opinion she was just a noisy, smelly nuisance. Life had been much easier before she arrived to clutter up the house.

Because baby Molly couldn't wander there, the garden became Daniel's refuge. He could practise his football skills, build leafy huts with Matt Pirelli, his friend from next door, and climb the oak tree. Best of all, though, was the big empty greenhouse which Daniel and Matt had turned into Starship Danmatt 1. They spent a whole weekend washing the glass panes and by the time they'd finished every pane sparkled like a diamond.

And then Grandpa Green arrived and that was that as far as the greenhouse was concerned. Grandpa Green took over.

Grandpa Green was Mrs Lloyd's father. When Granny Green died Mrs Lloyd decided that Grandpa should live with her, by which she meant with Mr Lloyd, Daniel and Molly as well. "Poor old Dad can't possibly live on his own," she said. "He can't even cook an egg." Daniel was suspicious. *He* could cook an egg so why couldn't an old man of seventy? He'd had sixty extra years to learn.

It didn't seem to bother Mrs Lloyd that her father was, to put it mildly, rather dirty. He was a tall, stringy man with long arms and flappy, soft hands. His fingernails always had mud or green stuff tucked beneath them and his nose dripped constantly. What remained of his hair curled over the back of his collar in long, grey tendrils.

Daniel had been very fond of his grandmother. She was a kind, thoughtful old lady. Whenever Daniel went to see her she would say, "Wrap up, Danny boy. We don't want you catching a cold, do we? Wrap up." Which was more than anyone else said, now that baby Molly was around.

So Daniel thought he had a right to know exactly what had happened to Granny Green. The last time he'd seen her she'd looked pretty fit. She'd even chased him round the house, for fun.

They were having a family tea when Daniel put the question. It was Grandpa Green's first day and he'd settled in well. He had a very good appetite.

Mrs Lloyd was pouring the tea when Daniel asked, "What exactly happened to Granny Green? I mean, why did she die?"

There was a deadly silence. You could have heard a pin drop if Mrs Lloyd hadn't forgotten to lift the teapot and so flooded all the saucers.

"Have I said something wrong?"

No one answered. Mrs Lloyd looked

anxiously at her father, while Mr Lloyd stared
at his plate of pilchards. A strange whistling
sound escaped Grandpa Green's sandy-
coloured teeth. He pulled a bit of celery out
of his mouth and laid it on his plate and
then he blew his nose on a
very dirty handkerchief.

Mr Lloyd took pity on his son. Leaning
close to Daniel he whispered, "Your grandma
disappeared."

Daniel was thrilled. He'd never known anyone who had disappeared. And then he began to worry. Suppose Granny Green wasn't dead? Suppose she'd been kidnapped or abducted by extraterrestrials. Of course, he had to ask. "So how d'you know she's dead?" He looked at his grandfather.

Grandpa Green chewed on a crust and looked over Daniel's head with a glazed expression.

"Of course she's dead," said Mrs Lloyd, who was Granny Green's daughter, after all. "Otherwise we wouldn't have had a funeral, would we?"

Daniel didn't know there'd been a funeral.

He wondered when they'd had it. Probably while he was at school. He felt cheated. "But if Granny disappeared that means there'd be no body. So how do you know she's—"

"The subject's closed!" said Mrs Lloyd.

Once again, Mr Lloyd took pity on Daniel. "They found a note," he whispered, "and a pile of clothes at the edge of a cliff. The police told us it was best to give up hope."

"What was under the cliff?" Daniel asked his father.

"The deep, deep sea!" came the answer, in a whisper.

So that was that.

"What was in the note?"

Mr Lloyd was about to tell Daniel when his wife said, "It's rude to whisper. Specially when there's a bereaved person sitting right in front of you."

Mr Lloyd and Daniel both said, "Sorry" and looked at Grandpa Green.

Grandpa Green washed down a mouthful of chips with his tea, burped and stood up. "I'll get on into the garden now," he said and he wandered out, wiping his sticky hands on the back of his combat trousers. Talking about Granny Green hadn't seemed to worry him in the slightest.

When he'd gone, Mr Lloyd winked at Daniel and said, "Goodbye."

Daniel was confused. Neither he nor his father had finished their tea.

"It's what Granny's note said," Mr Lloyd told him. "Goodbye."

Mrs Lloyd's head shot up. She'd been trying

to wipe something very yucky from the bottom of her father's plate. Chewing gum by the look of it. "You will not discuss my father and mother any more," she said. "You've never liked Dad, so if you can't find anything nice to say about him, don't say anything at all. It's bad enough having a tragedy in the family without people picking over it."

It was a tragedy all right. But it was also a mystery in Daniel's opinion. Why would a perfectly fit and, as far as he could tell, happy old lady take off her clothes and jump into the sea? It didn't make sense. Daniel resolved to get to the bottom of things.

Ignoring his father's frown, Daniel persevered. "There's just one thing I'd like to know . . ."

Mrs Lloyd scowled at Daniel, looking like a lioness about to roar. Luckily, at that moment baby Molly woke up from her afternoon nap and gave a bloodcurdling yell from upstairs. She always did this when she woke up. Daniel had come to the conclusion that the things she ate off the floor, which were numerous and disgusting, probably gave her nightmares.

Mrs Lloyd rushed out and Mr Lloyd said, "I should give the granny-thing a rest, Daniel. Mum's very upset about it. We don't want to drive her over the edge, do we?"

"Someone drove Granny over the edge," muttered Daniel.

He ran into the garden to do some thinking in

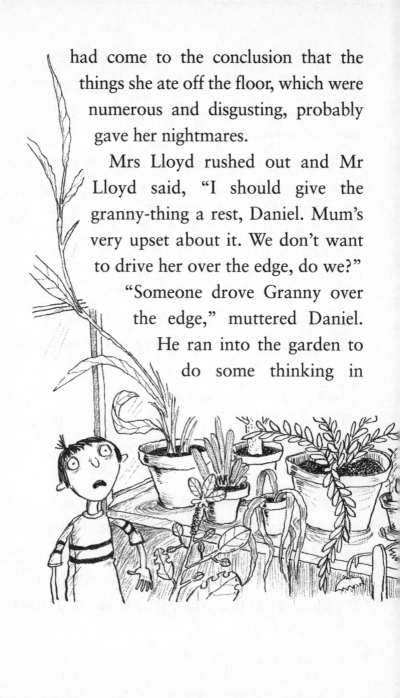

the quiet and empty greenhouse.

He was in for a shock. It wasn't an empty greenhouse any more. It was crammed full with plants. There they sat, in long rows of terracotta pots. The shelves could hardly be seen for greenery: long, trailing, leafy vines; curling, creeping, slimy stems; spiky plump things; thick multicoloured ferns and, right at the end, a gigantic, leafy tower that

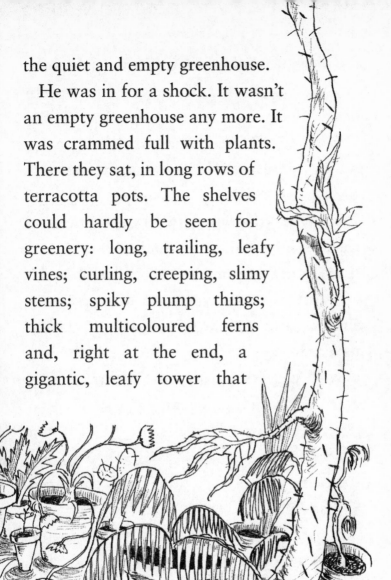

was already slinking across the glass roof. Starship Danmatt 1 had been invaded by aliens.

"Wha . . .!" Daniel's mouth fell open but nothing more would come out, it was such a shock.

"What're you doing in my greenhouse?" said a husky voice behind him.

Daniel nearly jumped out of his skin. He peered over his shoulder and his eyes met a yellowy-green stare. "Grandpa . . ." Daniel quavered.

"Well, you little toad, what're you doing in here?" said Grandpa Green.

"It's my place," Daniel said. "It's Starship Danmatt 1."

"Not now it isn't," said Grandpa Green. "Skidaddle!"

"But . . . but . . ." Daniel's mind was racing. Tomorrow Matt would come round with loads of equipment for their next mission. They'd been looking forward to it all week.

"Skidaddle!" Grandpa's blotchy face loomed closer.

Daniel decided it would be wise to retreat. He went up to his room and spent the afternoon watching the garden from his bedroom window. Grandpa Green was very busy. He was lining up hundreds of little pots outside the greenhouse. Now he was filling them with earth. Now he was pouring a brown liquid on to the earth, and now he was pressing little twigs into each pot. He seemed to be muttering to them.

Daniel waited for Grandpa Green to come indoors, so that he could go out for a last breath of fresh air. But the old man never came in, not even for his tea. He just went on potting and muttering.

"What's Grandpa doing out there?" Daniel asked his mother.

"Grandpa's going to make us a real

garden," said Mrs Lloyd. "Isn't it wonderful? We'll have vegetables and flowers and a lovely lawn."

No, it wasn't wonderful. Not when Starship Danmatt 1 had been taken over. Not when all the secret, leafy places in the garden had been invaded by a bossy old man. Daniel didn't like to say all this and drive his troubled mother over the edge. So he just muttered, "Hmm."

That night something woke Daniel up. Perhaps cats had been fighting outside or a fox had got into the garden. If he'd had a nightmare, he couldn't remember what it was. He sat up and looked out of the window.

At the bottom of the garden, lights flickered behind the great leafy plants in the greenhouse. Their shadows swung and hovered across the grass outside. One of the shadows had the head and shoulders of a human being. Daniel stifled a scream. It must be

14

Grandpa Green. But what was he doing out there in the middle of the night? Did he sleep with his plants?

Chapter 2
Stanley Disappears

"What's that?" said Daniel.

Grandpa Green was walking past the open back door with a lumpy brown sack. It was only half-past six in the morning. Daniel had got up specially early so that he could have his breakfast and get into the garden to investigate before his grandfather woke up.

"It's for my children." Grandpa Green gave Daniel a nasty smile. The smell from the sack was overpowering; like dead animals and sick.

Daniel found that he'd gone off his cereal. He couldn't manage another mouthful. He was sure one of the lumpy bits in the sack was moving. "What children?" he asked.

"My plants, Toad. It's plant food."

"Why d'you keep calling me a toad?"

"Because you look like one." Grandpa Green gave a loud chuckle and heaved the sack in the direction of the greenhouse.

Daniel felt angry and defeated. It didn't seem like his house any more, with a baby cluttering up the inside and an old man mucking about on the outside. All his quiet places had been stolen.

By the time Matt arrived, Daniel had worked himself into a fury. And fury made him brave, especially now that Matt was here. They'd show that nasty old man what boys were made of.

Unfortunately, Matt didn't feel brave. Grown-ups frightened him. He was disappointed to hear that the starship had been taken over, but he didn't feel like tackling a scary-sounding old man.

"Old men are quite strong these days," Matt told Daniel. "My mum says it's all the vitamins they take, and they do press-ups and jogging, and all sorts of things to give them big muscles. He's not violent, is he?"

"I don't know," Daniel admitted. "He's only been here a day. But he's no match for us." He picked up the box of goodies Matt had brought round. There were bicycle helmets, a wheel, a can of silver paint, a sheet, telephone cords, empty tins and jars, a goldfish bowl, a lamp shade and, best of all, an old grey boilersuit.

Matt stood by the kitchen door and watched Daniel striding down the garden.

"Come on, Matt!" called Daniel.

Matt didn't look at all confident and Daniel had a nasty feeling that his friend wasn't going to be much use in the forthcoming battle with Grandpa Green.

Where was his grandfather? The old man was nowhere to be seen. Matt began to cross the garden as though it were a minefield. He kept stopping to look in bushes and peer at the ground.

"He's not a mole," shouted Daniel.

"Who's not a mole?" Grandpa Green sprang out of the greenhouse. And then he turned and did something despicable. He locked the greenhouse door.

"You can't do that!" cried Daniel.

"I've just done it," sneered the old man.

Daniel put down the box and stared at the shiny new padlock screwed to the greenhouse door. "But we were going in there today. My friend's brought loads of stuff round specially."

Grandpa Green looked in the box and shook his head. "Come here, you!" He waggled a finger at the terrified Matt.

Matt crept closer.

"What's this?" Grandpa Green pointed at the box.

"It's . . . it's . . . ahem . . ." Matt cleared his throat, which seemed to have become clogged up with something. "It's things for our starship."

"Oh no it's not!" The old man poked Matt in the chest. "You can tell your mum she's not going to off-load all her old junk on us, thank you very much."

"It's not junk," said Daniel angrily.

Grandpa Green ignored him. He poked Matt in the chest again. "Now you can just pick up your festering rubbish and crawl back home to your miserable hovel, you slug," he said. And then, to Daniel's horror, he swore at him.

Matt's mouth hung open. He'd never met such a rude old man in his whole life. Grandpa Green had confirmed all his worst fears about grown-ups. Tears of shock stung his eyes, but he picked up the box and, for a moment, bravely stood his ground.

"I will go," he said, "and I'm never coming back."

"Matt . . ." begged Daniel.

"Never, never, never," cried Matt. He turned and raced across the garden, as fast as a boy with a heavy box could be expected to race.

"Matt!" Daniel tore after him.

"Don't come near me!" said Matt. He'd reached the gate and when he was safely through it, he shouted, "Your grandfather is a toxic pig. Why didn't you tell me?"

Daniel watched his terrified friend run home, and then he stormed back to his grandfather.

"How could you be so mean?" he cried. "You've taken my best place and now you've driven my best friend away." And suddenly words he hadn't known were there popped out of Daniel's mouth. "I don't believe my granny took off her clothes and jumped into the sea. I think you did something to her."

For a split second a look of panic crossed Grandpa Green's face. It was only a moment but Daniel reckoned he'd hit a nail on the head.

"Ooooooo!" said his grandfather in mock

horror. "D'you think her ghostie's going to haunt me, then?"

Daniel marched back into the house. Bad news awaited him. His parents were going out for the day and Grandpa Green was going to be in charge.

"You can't leave baby Molly with Grandpa!" Daniel was appalled. "I mean, he's just not the right sort of person for a baby."

"Don't be silly," said his mother. "Grandpa loves babies."

As it happened, Grandpa didn't even *like* babies and he soon made this very clear. When he heard that he was to babysit for a whole day he got very red in the face and shouted, "Me? Not on your nelly. I'm not looking after it."

"Oh come on, Dad, why not?" pleaded Mrs Lloyd.

"Don't like the way it screams. Don't like the way it crawls under your feet. Worst of

all, I don't like the way it puts things in its mouth. Any old things."

"She's not an it, she's Molly," said a tearful Mrs Lloyd. She'd been looking forward to her day out so much.

"I'll look after her," Daniel offered, afraid that she might go over the edge.

"You can't," sniffed Mrs Lloyd. "You're too young."

Mr Lloyd had a brilliant idea. "How about Lorna? She'll do anything for money."

"Your sister?" Mrs Lloyd looked doubtful.

"She's very irresponsible, and she's got that nasty little dog."

"A dog?" yelped Grandpa Green. "I won't have a dog in my garden and that's flat."

"Look here, Dad, either you look after Molly or we'll have to ask Lorna." Mrs Lloyd was at last beginning to lose her temper with her father.

Grandpa Green made a rude growling noise and stomped off.

In less than an hour Lorna and Stanley were on the doorstep. Stanley was a small white mongrel with long fluffy hair. He wore a bright red collar studded with sparkling stones.

"Hello, sweetheart!" said Lorna when Daniel opened the door to his favourite aunt. "Auntie Lorna's come to babysit. Aren't you the lucky one?"

She teetered past him in high-heeled sandals that exactly matched Stanley's collar. In her tight red skirt and tight black jumper, with sequins in her blonde hair and silver on her eyelids, Daniel reckoned she was the nearest thing to a popstar he'd ever meet. He hoped baby Molly wouldn't be sick on her.

It turned out that Lorna was very good with babies. She was soon throwing Molly in the air and catching her, singing nursery rhymes and playing with bricks.

Grandpa Green had vanished. Daniel guessed he was in the greenhouse, sulking.

When Lorna took off Stanley's lead and let him run loose in the garden, Daniel was worried.

"Grandpa Green doesn't like dogs," he warned Lorna. "He might do something nasty to Stanley."

"I'd like to see him try," said Lorna. "Come on, sweetheart, let's make some chocolate brownies."

They spent a very enjoyable half hour in the kitchen, eating chocolate and butter and nuts, before they got down to the cooking. It was a warm, sunny day, so they left the back door wide open. The brownies had just gone in the oven when Stanley tore into the kitchen and jumped into Lorna's arms, whining and whimpering. Grandpa Green burst in after him.

"That piece of garbage, that hound from hell, he's just peed against my greenhouse door," he roared. "I'll kill the louse."

"How dare you!" said sparky Lorna. "Stanley's my treasure. And look at you. You're filthy. Don't think you're going to get a chocolate brownie looking like that."

"I hate chocolate brownies!" spat Grandpa Green. "I hate 'em almost as much as I hate dogs." He was looking straight at Stanley when he said this and there was a deadly gleam in his eyes as he crashed out through the door.

Daniel should have taken more notice of that gleam in his grandfather's eyes. By the time he remembered, it was too late. Much too late.

He was never quite sure how Stanley got out again. He thought he had shut the back door, but perhaps he hadn't. Perhaps someone else had opened it, ever so quietly. All he knew was that, suddenly, Stanley wasn't there.

Lorna called Stanley's name all over the house. But there was no answering bark. Only Molly singing, "Sta-leeee! Sta-leeee!"

Lorna and Daniel went into the garden and called again. "Stanley! Stanley!"

"He always comes when I call him." Lorna's eyes were beginning to go red; a watery blob of mascara trickled down her cheek.

Daniel hated seeing perky Lorna looking so desperate. He felt it was all his fault. And then he noticed that the greenhouse door was open. He rushed across the garden, his heart pounding.

There was no sign of Stanley in the greenhouse. Not that Daniel could see much. Grandpa Green's plants had grown astonishingly in a single day. Their leafy stems snaked across the glass, blotting out the light. Even the roof was covered with sinewy green stalks.

Daniel squinted into the shadows. "Stanley?" he whispered. The towering plants seemed to forbid normal speech. In the murky gloom they looked much more like hunched monsters than normal plants. Daniel had a nasty suspicion that they were watching him.

He didn't want to walk further into the greenhouse, but he felt he had to, for Lorna's sake. As he moved a hissing, swishing sound swept round him. The plants were whispering, and was it his imagination or did a quiet voice say, "Wrap up, Danny boy!"

At the end of the greenhouse he found the biggest plant of all. Its smell was so disgusting Daniel had to pinch his nose. He could see the glint of something liquid oozing down the stem: a thick green slime. Daniel felt sick. He bent over and retched. This was worse than any flu bug.

And then he saw Stanley's red collar. It was

lying right at his feet. It had been snapped in two by razor-sharp teeth. Bits of green slime clung to the sparkly studs.

Daniel grabbed the collar and rushed to the door. He couldn't open it. No matter how hard he kicked and pushed, the door was stuck fast.

"Help! Help! Help!" Daniel shouted.

The plants didn't like that. They didn't like that at all. The chorus of whispers intensified. It became an angry, buzzing ocean of sound.

"Help!" whimpered Daniel, sinking to his knees.

Chapter 3
Advice from Matt

"Sweetheart!"

Daniel blinked.

Lorna was staring at him from the open door of the greenhouse. "Are you all right, sweetheart?"

"I got locked in," Daniel croaked.

"Did you?" Lorna helped him to his feet.

"Yes, I think Grandpa must have locked the door."

"It wasn't locked when I got here," said Lorna. "You look very pale, sweetheart."

"I felt sick," said Daniel. "I know I left the door open, but when I got to it, it was shut." He held up Stanley's collar. "But look, I found Stanley's collar."

Lorna's hand flew to her mouth. She grabbed the collar. "Oh, my poor Stanley. It's been chewed through."

"As if by a monster!"

"Oh, Daniel, don't. Whatever could it be?"

"Who knows?" Daniel couldn't bring himself to tell Lorna about the slimy plant. "It's very dark in there." He pointed into the gloom behind him. "Maybe a Rottweiler or a Dobermann got in. You know, a vicious type of dog that eats other dogs."

"What?" Lorna looked stunned. "A dog wouldn't do that to another dog, would it?" She didn't seem too sure. "I'm going to have a look."

"I wouldn't if I were you," warned Daniel.

It was too late. Lorna was already in. "This place stinks," she said. "Ugh!" A pot fell over, and then another.

"Auntie Lorna, please come out," begged

Daniel. "Grandpa Green doesn't like people going in the greenhouse."

Where was Grandpa Green? Was he hiding in the shrubbery or spying on them from his room? And why hadn't he locked the green-house?

Lorna came stumbling out, holding a broken pot. "I've knocked something over," she said. "I couldn't see a thing in there. It's horrible. Spooky and smelly. I'm going to ring the police."

"About the greenhouse?"

"There's no law against smelly green-houses," said Lorna. "No, I'm going to tell them about Stanley. Just in case . . ." she began to look tearful again, "in case a little body has been found."

There was a sudden, loud bellow from the gate and Grandpa Green came staggering through with another big sack full of some-thing.

"Get away from my plants," he yelled.

"Keep your hair on," shouted Lorna. "I'm only looking for my poor little dog. Have you seen him?"

"No. I haven't." Grandpa Green lurched up to them and dumped his sack beside the greenhouse. "What's that?" He glared at the piece of broken pottery in Lorna's hand.

"I'm afraid I knocked something over."

"You what?" roared Grandpa Green. He disappeared into the greenhouse.

"I'll go and see my friend next door," Daniel told Lorna. "Stanley might have got through the hedge."

"Thank you, sweetheart." Lorna brushed away a tear. "You're a good boy."

Baby Molly began to howl and Lorna rushed into the house, while Daniel walked round to see Matt.

"Matt's rather upset," said Mrs Pirelli when she saw Daniel on the doorstep.

"I know," said Daniel. "Can I come in and talk to him?"

Mrs Pirelli gave a big shrug. "You're welcome to try. I don't know what's wrong with him. He rushed upstairs this morning muttering something about old people and hasn't come down since."

"It's my grandpa," said Daniel. "He was a bit rude."

"Oh?" Mrs Pirelli rolled her eyes. "Go on, then, see if you can cheer Matt up."

Daniel climbed the stairs and knocked on Matt's door.

"What?" said Matt's sulky voice.

"It's me. Daniel. Can I come in?"

"All right."

Matt was sitting in the middle of the floor,

surrounded by all the things that should have been in Starship Danmatt 1. He looked very depressed.

Daniel crouched beside him and picked up the silver paint. "Silver would have looked great," he said.

Matt nodded. "*Would've*. We could have put it all over the shelves and the helmets and all the tins and things."

"I'm sorry about Grandpa," said Daniel. "But I've got to live with him for ever, as far as I can see. Imagine what that's going to be like."

"I can't, it's too horrible." Matt gave a grim smile. "Tell you what, though, I've been sitting here thinking and I had this idea, so I asked Dad and he said yes."

"What was your idea?"

"A tent," said Matt. "We could put all this stuff in a tent, paint it silver and everything, and it would be just as good as the green-house. What d'you think?"

"Brilliant!" said Daniel.

They sat and discussed the new starship for a long time, both of them feeling a lot happier than they had an hour ago. It wasn't until Daniel decided he'd better get back to Lorna and Molly  that he remembered why he'd come. He told Matt about disappearing Stanley and the horrible whispering plants. "I know Grandpa's got something to do with Stanley disappearing," he said. "He's admitted he hates dogs, and there was Stanley's red collar, bitten right through, with all this slimy stuff on it."

Matt looked thoughtful. He was good with ideas. At last he said, "I know it'll be difficult, but if you pretend to be nice to your grandpa, you know, pretend you're on his side, then he might tell you something . . . about the plants."

"Hmm." Being nice to Grandpa Green wouldn't be easy, but it was worth a try. "I'll tell you how I get on," said Daniel. "Thanks for the advice."

"Good luck! See you!" Matt gave the thumbs up sign.

When Daniel got home the house was unusually quiet. He found Grandpa Green in the kitchen, eating chocolate brownies.

 "I thought you said you didn't like those," said Daniel, forgetting Matt's advice.

"I'm only eating them to please Lorna," said the old man with a grumpy pout.

"Oh? Where is Lorna?"

"Gone home," said Grandpa Green. "But I told her before she left that I'd eat some brownies."

Daniel was very surprised. "But what about baby Molly?"

"She forgot about poor Molly." Grandpa Green sighed. "Young women these days. I don't know. All she could talk about was that pesky hound, that interfering dirty pooch." He burped and stuffed the last brownie into his mouth. "*I've* been looking after baby Molly."

This time Daniel was more than surprised, he was downright suspicious.

"You?" He ran up to Molly's room and peered into her cot. She was lying on her back fast asleep. A thin trickle of brown stuff ran from the corner of her mouth across her cheek and on to her pillow. Daniel tore down to the kitchen.

"What've you given our baby?" he cried. "There's some horrible stuff coming out of her mouth. It looks like the stuff I saw you feeding the plants."

"Calm down, Danny!" said his grandfather. "I gave her the teeny-weeniest bit of chocolate to cheer her up. Now, d'you want Grandpa to cook you something?"

"I thought you couldn't cook," Daniel said, rather too quickly. Why was the old man being nice all of a sudden? He remembered Matt's advice and, after a terrible struggle with himself, he managed to say, "Thanks all the same, but I'm not hungry."

Molly was still asleep when Mr and Mrs Lloyd came home. This was very puzzling, but not as puzzling as the news that Lorna had left.

"I can't believe she went off like that," said Mrs Lloyd. "Thank goodness Grandpa was here. Anything could have happened to you and Molly."

"I'm not paying her for a whole day's babysitting and that's flat," said Mr Lloyd. "She promised to stay until we got back."

"She lost Stanley," Daniel told them. "She

42

was really worried because I found his collar in the greenhouse and it was chewed right through."

Grandpa Green gave Daniel a nasty stare. "Dogs," he muttered. "Pests, that's what they are."

The doorbell rang and Mrs Lloyd said, "That'll be Lorna. I expect she just popped out for a bit of shopping."

Daniel went to answer the door. It wasn't Lorna. It was her boyfriend, Eric, who was in rather a state. "Where's Lorna?" he said. "I've been ringing her mobile for ages, but she won't answer. She said she'd be here."

"I think she went home," said Daniel.

"No, she didn't," said Eric. "I've just been there and no one's in."

"Oh." A frightening image popped into Daniel's head. He saw a pile of Lorna's clothes on a clifftop. The note pinned to her skirt said:

Goodbye. I can't live without Stanley.

Of course, Daniel couldn't tell Eric anything about this terrible imaginary picture. Eric would be heart-broken on two counts. One, because there was no Lorna. Two, because she'd loved a dog more than him. Pulling himself together, Daniel told Eric to come in for a cup of tea.

Chapter 4
Lorna's Shoes

It was Grandpa Green who finally shed light on the mystery of Lorna's disappearance. They were sitting around the kitchen table, Mr and Mrs Lloyd, Eric, Grandpa and Daniel. Molly was still in an unusually deep sleep.

Eric sipped his tea, looking more anxious every minute and then, with a big sigh, Grandpa Green said, "I hate to be the one to break the news."

Everyone put down their cups of tea and stared at Grandpa, waiting.

The old man scratched the back of his head, then his ears and nose, burped quietly and said, "There's another man, Eric."

"What?" Eric's eyes nearly popped out of his head. "I don't believe it."

"I'm sorry," said Grandpa Green. "But I couldn't help overhearing. Lorna must've rung him at least three times. 'Oh, Bruce,' she kept saying. 'I love you so much.'" Grandpa put on a funny, high voice that was supposed to sound like Lorna's, but was actually much closer to Stanley's bark.

"Bruce who?" Eric stood up, knocking over his cup. "I've never heard of a Bruce."

"I don't know, do I?" whined Grandpa Green. "She just said, 'I'll meet you on the corner in five minutes,' and then she was gone."

Eric rushed out crying, "What am I going to do? What'll become of me? I can't live without Lorna."

"A very flimsy young man," Grandpa Green remarked as the front door slammed. "No backbone."

"Why didn't you tell us all about this Bruce person before?" asked Mrs Lloyd.

"Didn't think it was any of my business," said Grandpa Green. He stomped out to the garden, looking offended.

That night Daniel found it impossible to sleep. He didn't believe a word that his grandfather had said. It was all lies, every bit of it. There was no such person as Bruce. Lorna had never left the house. She wouldn't. But where was she? And where was Stanley? Tomorrow Daniel would try again to put Matt's plan into action. He would start being nice to Grandpa Green. But it would be hard. Very hard.

In the middle of the night baby Molly woke up howling, and Daniel could honestly say that he was very happy to hear those baby wails. He'd had a terrible suspicion that Grandpa Green had given Molly something to make her sleep for ever.

*

"I don't know what you gave Molly to eat yesterday," Mrs Lloyd said at breakfast next morning, "but she's got a tremendous appetite."

"Just a little bit of chocolate," said Grandpa Green innocently.

"Oh, Dad, you know you shouldn't—" She was interrupted by a loud crash from the garden.

CRASH! CLANK! CLATTER! CLANG!

"What the—?" Mr Lloyd ran to the kitchen window. "Holy Moses!" he exclaimed.

Everyone crowded behind him and looked into the garden.

An astonishing sight met their eyes. A plant had smashed its way through the top of the greenhouse. Bits of broken glass lay every-where and a towering green stem with big fleshy leaves lurched crazily over the roof.

"Oh, my! Oh, Lor! It's the Bodigulpa!" Grandpa Green opened the back door and tore down to the greenhouse.

Daniel was hot on his heels.

"Mind that glass!" called Mrs Lloyd. "It'll have to be cleared up."

Grandpa Green unlocked the door and went into the greenhouse. Daniel followed.

"Oh, my lovely! My prize, my treasure, have you had too much protein?" The old man rushed to the end of the greenhouse where the roots of the huge plant seemed to be bursting through their pot. The stem had thickened by at least ten centimetres.

"What was that word you said, Grandpa?" asked Daniel. "Bodi . . . something."

His grandfather looked down as if he'd only just become aware that Daniel was there. "Bodigulpa," he said. "That's its name."

Daniel whispered. "Weird. Who named it?"

"I did. I created it," his grandfather said proudly. "It's not like other plants. It's special. It eats . . ."

"What?" asked Daniel. "Eats what? Bodies?" He giggled. "Only joking."

Grandpa Green rubbed his chin as if he were sizing Daniel up, as if he might be thinking about telling his grandson a secret. But he said nothing. He just set about tidying the bits of broken glass and scattered earth.

"I'll get a dustpan and brush," Daniel offered.

"It needs support," said his grandfather. "See, it's too tall for its own good."

"Why did it grow so quickly?"

"Like I said," murmured the old man. "Too much protein. It's had a big meal."

Daniel felt a bit queasy but he knew he had to keep pretending to be nice to Grandpa. "You could use the pole from the washing-line," he suggested. "That might support your . . . Bodigulpa."

Grandpa Green darted him a look. "You're not as stupid as you look, Toad!"

Daniel wasn't sure if this was flattering or

not. He ran off to fetch the dustpan and brush, while Grandpa Green went to beg Mrs Lloyd for the loan of her washing-line pole.

Now that it had lost part of its roof, there was more light in the greenhouse, and it wasn't so stuffy and smelly. The creepers that had been curling across the glass top had fallen out and were drooping helplessly over the sides.

Daniel knelt on the grimy floor and began to sweep up the broken glass. It wasn't the sort of thing he'd have chosen to do on a Sunday morning, but it was being nice to Grandpa Green. Perhaps the old man would trust him enough to tell him what really happened to Lorna. And Stanley. And Granny.

He was thinking of his grandmother when a voice whispered, "Wrap up, Danny boy!" Was it his imagination? The whispering had begun again; a rustling, muttering, sinister chorus surged around him. From somewhere at the back of the greenhouse there came a distant, doggy whine, and then, more distinctly, the ring of a mobile phone.

"I'm getting out of here," Daniel murmured.

And then he saw the shoe. Two shoes. Red sandals with very high heels. They were lying behind the huge pot that held the Bodigulpa.

With trembling fingers Daniel pulled them out. A thick, gluey substance clung to the narrow straps.

"What've you got there, Toad?" said a voice behind him.

Daniel almost leapt out of his skin. He hadn't heard Grandpa Green's soft foot-falls. "It's Auntie Lorna's shoes," Daniel said in a shaky voice. "H-how did they get here?"

"Cowhide!" said Grandpa Green.

"What?"

"Cowhide. Leather to you. It doesn't like leather."

53

"What doesn't?" said Daniel, completely baffled and rather frightened.

"The Bodigulpa," said Grandpa Green.

Chapter 5
A Fight

"Look!" Daniel held up the red sandals. "They're Auntie Lorna's."

"Good grief!" Mrs Lloyd practically dropped baby Molly. "Why did she leave them in the greenhouse? And what's that stuff on them?"

"Sooze!" said Molly, stretching out a hand.

Daniel didn't even want to think about how Lorna's shoes had got into the greenhouse or how they had come to be hidden behind the Bodigulpa. He had just clutched the shoes and run away from Grandpa Green as fast as his legs would carry him. He wanted to do something about Lorna before Grandpa could start making up stories again.

"I think you should tell the police," Daniel told his mother. "Auntie Lorna's been kidnapped, or something."

"No, she hasn't, Daniel. You heard Grandpa; he said she went off to see her new boyfriend. Though why she took off her shoes, I can't imagine."

"Grandpa's lying!" cried Daniel.

"Daniel! Don't ever let me hear you say that again. Your own grandpa – my father. He doesn't tell lies." Mrs Lloyd was so agitated she dumped Molly on a chair that wasn't there.

"Yowl!" cried Molly, clinging to the edge of the table.

It crossed Daniel's mind that Molly got a rough deal sometimes. But there were other, more pressing, things on his mind at the moment. "What about Stanley?" he said.

"What about him?" Mrs Lloyd stamped her foot. "Really, Daniel, I've got enough to worry about without searching for a silly runaway dog. Molly's eating everything in sight. This morning she swallowed my precious cactus. Think of that!"

Daniel tried not to. The cactus was as big as his hand and had horrible spikes all down its sides.

"Hello! Hello!" Grandpa Green poked his head through the back door. "What's this? A little argument."

Daniel whirled round, still holding the red shoes.

"Ah, I suppose you've been worrying your mum about Auntie Lorna's shoes." Grandpa Green stumbled through the door. "Well, there's no need to fret. She was wearing some very sensible trainers when she went off to meet her new boyfriend. I expect she wanted to run, and you can't run in high heels, can you?" He gave a throaty chuckle.

"There!" said Mrs Lloyd. "I knew there'd be a perfectly reasonable explanation."

Daniel dropped the shoes and walked out. He decided to lie low for a while. If Grandpa Green was going to get away with telling lies, there was no point in arguing.

That afternoon a storm blew up. The wind howled in the trees and rattled the doors and windows. The overgrown Bodigulpa, tied to its pole, thrashed above the greenhouse like an angry giant. Its long arms slapped the glass and even more panes fell out. The rain poured through the roof, drenching the plants inside.

Grandpa Green sat in the kitchen rubbing his chin. Occasionally he looked into the garden and shook his head. "Didn't know it'd come to this," he muttered.

Daniel, on his way to fetch a Mars bar, pricked up his ears. "Come to what, Grandpa?" With Matt's advice in mind he used a polite tone of voice.

"I didn't know it'd grow so quickly, did I? It's angry, see. Very angry. It hates the cold weather and it's so furious, it won't drink any of the potion I concocted to keep it calm."

"Why d'you think it grew so fast?" Daniel tried to sound casual. He sat at the table and unwrapped his Mars bar.

His grandfather stared at him with narrowed eyes. He drummed his fingers on the table and muttered something under his breath. Daniel chewed his Mars bar, pretending not to be too interested in what the old man had to say.

As a particularly vicious gust of wind hurled the watering can against the wall, Grandpa Green mumbled, "It's a carnivore."

"A carnivore?" Daniel knew very well what a carnivore was, he just wanted to make sure he'd heard right.

"A meat-eater," said Grandpa Green.

"The Bodigulpa?"

The old man nodded. "Yup. And some of the others."

"How did they get like that?"

Grandpa Green cleared his throat, and Daniel sensed that being friendly had paid off. His grandfather was about to reveal something.

"It gets a bit boring when you retire," said the old man. "You can go down the pub, have a laugh now and again, watch TV, mow the lawn. But it wasn't enough for me. I like to be active, so I started taking an interest in the garden. And then I got these jungle plants. I ordered them through the Internet." He looked out at the thrashing Bodigulpa and then continued pensively, "They were very keen on flies."

Daniel waited expectantly, but his grand-father seemed to have ground to a halt and Daniel didn't dare say a word to break the spell.

All of a sudden the old man roused himself and said solemnly, "That's how it began. Then I cross-pollinated, bred bigger plants. I grafted and fed. I nurtured and comforted. I even read them bedtime stories. They were particularly fond of *Jack and the Beanstalk*. Your grandmother was very put out. D'you know, I think she was jealous."

"Of a plant?" Daniel couldn't help saying.

"Yes, Daniel. She was jealous of my plants, said I spent too much time with them. By then

I was giving them mice three times a week. The pet shops in our area all ran out. So I had to think of something else. I tried raw steak, sausages, chicken, lamb chops, everything a butcher has to offer, but d'you know what?"

"No," said Daniel breathlessly.

"The Bodigulpa ruddy well chucked everything back at me."

"Even the sausages?" Daniel was so intrigued he didn't even stop to wonder *how* a plant could chuck something, let alone eat it.

"Even the sausages. The others aren't so fussy. It's the Bodigulpa. My favourite. It prefers things that are alive, you see. Your granny wasn't very sympathetic, I'm afraid. She said they all had to go; said they stank.

I ask you. They don't smell as bad as she did, the old bat."

Daniel was shocked. He'd always assumed his grandparents loved each other, not passionately of course, but in a fond and comfortable way. "Granny wasn't an old bat," he muttered. "She was a nice old lady."

"Huh!" Grandpa Green banged his fist on the table. "You don't know the half of it."

By now Daniel had a sinking feeling in the pit of his stomach. He wanted to ask more but dreaded what his grandfather might tell him.

Luckily, just then Mr Lloyd made a rather dramatic entrance, brandishing a pair of gardening shears. "You'll have to cut that plant down," he told Grandpa Green. "It's too big for the greenhouse."

"Cut the . . . cut my . . ." Grandpa Green went white. "Cut my . . ." he stuttered.

"Your plant. The big one. Look at it. It's rattling around on that pole. It'll smash up the whole greenhouse. Besides, we want the pole back."

"It can't be cut!" Grandpa Green got to his feet, nervously wringing his grimy hands.

"It'll grow again," said Mr Lloyd. "It just needs a bit of pruning."

"Would you grow again if your head was chopped off?" Grandpa Green demanded.

"Don't be silly," said Mr Lloyd. "It's hardly Mary Queen of Scots. Plants aren't human beings. And we can't mend the roof with that thing sticking out of the top."

"It can't eat if it hasn't got a head!" yelled Grandpa Green.

"Come off it, Grandpa!" Mr Lloyd opened the back door. "I'll do it if you won't."

"Over my dead body!"

With amazing speed and agility, Grandpa Green leapt in front of Mr Lloyd. His big hands were bunched into tight, knobbly fists. He lunged left, right, left again.

Mr Lloyd stared at his father-in-law in

astonishment. He couldn't decide what to do. Unfortunately he made the wrong decision. He put one foot forward.

SOCK! Grandpa Green punched him in the eye.

"Ow!"

Mr Lloyd staggered backwards, dropping the shears.

"That gave you a fright, didn't it, Barry Lloyd?" cried Grandpa Green, skipping gleefully round Mr Lloyd. "Not so pleased with ourselves now, are we?"

Clutching his bruised eye with one hand, Mr Lloyd clenched the other and advanced on Grandpa Green.

At this point, Daniel wondered if he ought to step between the two angry men, but he thought better of it. They were both a lot bigger than he was and besides, he was interested in the outcome of the fight. His father was younger, but was he fitter?

CRUNCH! Mr Lloyd landed a blow on the old man's chin.

SOCK! Grandpa Green went for Mr Lloyd's other eye.

This was too much for Mr Lloyd. With a bloodthirsty growl, he seized a frying pan and smashed it against his father-in-law's head.

"Awwww!" The old man sank to the floor like a stone.

"Well done, Dad!" said Daniel.

Father and son stared down at the old man spreadeagled on the kitchen floor.

"What're you going to do now, Dad?" asked Daniel.

"I'm going to cut down that plant," said Mr Lloyd.

Chapter 6
The Bodigulpa's Revenge

"So what happened yesterday?" asked Matt.

"It's a long story," said Daniel. "My auntie Lorna and her dog disappeared and Dad and Grandpa had a fight."

"Whew!" whistled Matt.

The two boys had just managed to grab five minutes alone in the school break.

"Dad won. He knocked Grandpa out. When he came round, he seemed different, a bit scared and quiet."

"So he's not as tough as he thinks he is. Did you get anything out of him?"

"Yes," Daniel said grimly, "and I think . . . I know it's hard to believe, but . . . I think," he took a breath, "I think one of his plants has eaten my auntie and her dog."

Matt's jaw dropped. "You're joking!"

Daniel solemnly shook his head. "I'm not." He told Matt about the Bodigulpa and its nasty eating habits.

"But it couldn't eat a *person*," Matt protested. "People are too big, and it'd need a mouth and teeth."

"I think it's got them – somewhere," Daniel said. "And it's as wide as a person now. You ought to see it. It smashed its way through the roof of the greenhouse and Dad was going to chop its head off, but Mum said he shouldn't because it would upset Grandpa too much, so he got a ladder and snipped some of the leaves off and then pulled the top back into the greenhouse. It looks horrible now." Daniel shuddered, remembering the great head drooping from its thick stem.

"I wish I could see it."

"Come round after tea," said Daniel.

Matt looked doubtful. "Is your grandpa

still, you know – quiet? You don't think he'll be so angry?"

"I don't know. I didn't see him this morning. You can always go home if he gets rough."

"OK."

The bell went and they ran back to their classroom.

When Daniel got home later that afternoon, Grandpa Green was out.

"Is he going to be out for a long time?" Daniel asked hopefully.

"Goodness knows," said Mrs Lloyd. "He's been very down today. He said he was going to the park to cheer himself up."

"The park?" Daniel wondered what could be cheerful about a park on such a grey, drizzly day?

"Be a love and keep an eye on baby Molly, will you?" His mother pulled on her raincoat. "I've got to pop down to the shops to get something for tea. I won't be a sec."

"You're usually hours at the shops," Daniel complained. "And you said I was too young to babysit."

"Look, this isn't babysitting. It's five minutes keeping an eye open. Your dad'll be home soon and I want to get some fruit cake." Mrs Lloyd whizzed out of the front door before Daniel could say another word.

He found Molly playing with her blue teddy on the kitchen floor. Daniel joined in the game. He built a wall of bricks round the teddy but it fell in a heap when Molly tried to help. "Hungree!" she said. Daniel wondered if he should give her something to eat.

He was just opening the fridge door when Grandpa Green staggered in carrying a large plastic sack. The sack was full of something lumpy and slightly wriggly.

"More plant food?" Daniel asked.

"Yup." Grandpa Green sat down breathing heavily. His face was very red and little beads of sweat dripped down the sides of his stubbly cheeks. "Phew! Had a bit of a work-out," he said, patting his heart. "Old ticker's not what it was."

"D'you want a drink of water?" Daniel asked. The old man looked as if he'd just run a marathon.

"Nope." Grandpa Green lurched to his feet. "Got to feed that plant or there'll be hell to pay." He grabbed the sack and dragged it through the back door. "It's been in a rage since your father chopped its leaves off."

Daniel found a pot of strawberry yoghurt, pulled off the top and handed it to Molly.

"Yum!" said baby Molly, burying her nose in it.

"Stay there, Molly," said Daniel. He felt a bit guilty as he opened the back door and stepped into the garden. But Molly looked quite safe, gobbling up yoghurt and feeding the blue teddy. And Daniel just *had* to find out how the Bodigulpa ate its food.

Daniel raced across the garden. Grandpa Green had already disappeared. The big plastic sack stood outside the greenhouse. As Daniel got closer, he heard a bark. It sounded just like Stanley. If Stanley had come back, perhaps Auntie Lorna would too. He thought he heard a voice. Was it Lorna's? There was no mistaking the next voice he heard. "Wrap up, Danny boy!" It was Granny Green's.

Daniel reached the greenhouse and looked in.

Grandpa Green was staring up at the Bodigulpa. Its long, thick neck looked bare and white, except for the pink stuff oozing from the stumps of its amputated leaves. The head was like a giant tulip with four tightly folded red petals. It hung over the old man, swaying slightly in the wind. But there was no wind. Mr Lloyd had covered the hole in the roof with a wide strip of sacking. The head was moving by itself.

"I'm sorry," said Grandpa Green. "It wasn't me. I tried to stop him. Does it hurt, dear?"

"Haaaaaa!" A dreadful hissing sound came from the head of the Bodigulpa. The tips of the petals turned back and several drops of liquid trickled on to the old man's head.

"Ouch!" Grandpa Green stepped back.

That's when Daniel saw the teeth. The big, red petals curled right back, like the lips of a snarling wolf, and there inside were two rows of long, saw-like teeth. As the ghastly mouth lunged down, it opened wider. Wider and wider. Grandpa Green stood rooted to the spot.

The other plants began to murmur and

mutter. Distant voices echoed through the leaves. Squeaks! Howls! Birdsong!

Daniel felt a scream inside him that couldn't be uttered.

"Forgive me," whispered Grandpa Green.

But the Bodigulpa wouldn't forgive. The huge mouth clamped over the old man's head and before Daniel could move, it had lifted Grandpa Green clean off his feet. For a brief moment his body swung in the air, and then it was gone; sucked up into the huge, red jaws.

As Daniel stood there, too terrified to move or speak, the great stem of the Bodigulpa collapsed. It crashed to the ground, its head twisting and writhing, and suddenly Grandpa Green's shoes shot out of its mouth. They lay at Daniel's feet in a pool of green slime.

"Aaaaah!" yelled Daniel. Leaping backwards, he found himself tumbling over the green sack. It rolled on to its side and a horde of squirrels bounded out. They began to swarm across the garden, hundreds of them,

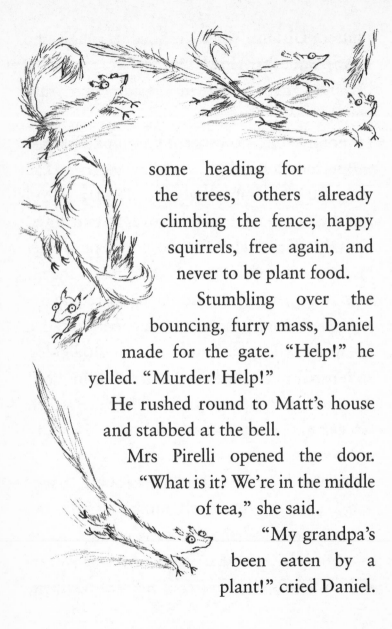

some heading for
the trees, others already
climbing the fence; happy
squirrels, free again, and
never to be plant food.

Stumbling over the
bouncing, furry mass, Daniel
made for the gate. "Help!" he
yelled. "Murder! Help!"

He rushed round to Matt's house
and stabbed at the bell.

Mrs Pirelli opened the door.
"What is it? We're in the middle
of tea," she said.

"My grandpa's
been eaten by a
plant!" cried Daniel.

"Don't be silly, Daniel," said Mrs Pirelli. "Come and have some cake."

She turned away and Daniel followed her into the kitchen. "It's true," he said. "Honestly! Mum and Dad are out. I don't know what to do."

"Daniel says his grandpa's been eaten by a plant," Mrs Pirelli told Matt. "I expect it's an alien." She giggled.

"It's not funny, Mum!" Matt jumped up from the table, his eyes very wide. "D'you want me to come round?"

Daniel nodded dumbly.

"You haven't finished your tea," grumbled Mrs Pirelli.

"This is urgent, Mum." The boys ran out into the street.

"Wait a minute," Matt said. "Tell me exactly what happened."

Daniel related the whole horrible story from the moment his grandfather appeared with a sack full of squirrels, until the

Bodigulpa spat out his shoes.

"He's gone for good, then," said Matt.

Daniel shrugged. "I suppose so. But then so have Lorna, and Stanley and . . . and I'm sure Granny Green's in there somewhere. In the plant I mean."

"No one's going to believe you," said Matt.

"No," Daniel agreed. "But there's always the shoes and the dog collar. That's sort of proof, isn't it?"

"Sort of. Let's go and see it."

Just as he was closing the back gate, Daniel remembered that he was supposed to be babysitting. Something caught his eye. It was Molly's blue teddy, lying beside the greenhouse door.

Daniel stared at Matt. "Our baby!" he said, then he was flying across the garden, yelling, "Molly! Molly! Come out! Molleeeee!"

Molly hadn't been eaten. Molly was just fine. She'd had a little feast. Out she came tottering towards Daniel on her sturdy little legs.

"Molly, you can walk!" cried Daniel, tears of relief springing to his eyes. "You clever, clever baby."

She was clutching two red petals and a bunch of dark leaves. And now Daniel could see that she was chewing something pale and slimy. There was a trickle of watery green stuff on her chin.

Molly beamed at Daniel. "Hello, sweetheart!" she said, in a voice that wasn't hers.

Daniel froze. He took in the red petals, the dark leaves, the green dribble. "Matt," he whispered. "I think Molly has eaten the Bodigulpa."

"She couldn't. Could she? How could a baby defeat a giant plant?"

Molly gave a hiccup that sounded suspiciously like a bark and then, in the tones of an elderly female, she said, "Wrap up, Danny boy! Wrap up."

The boys stared at her in horror. And then Molly did something that sent them screaming and howling away from her.

In a deep, crusty voice, Molly said, "What are you scared of, toads!"

Another book in the Shock Shop series . . .

Stealaway

K. M. Peyton

Gloomy, brooding Bloodybow Castle
– a place of ancient secrets . . .

Nicky's new home, Bloodybow Castle, is so
dark and forbidding. How can Nicky and
her mother live in such a spooky place?

But Nicky soon realizes that Bloodybow is
haunted by a terrible past. Hundreds of
years ago, border raiders stole a priceless
stallion, starting a feud that led to the death
of a young boy.

And now strange events surround
Bloodybow once more. A white pony
mysteriously comes and goes. Eerie lights
are seen at night. And then Stealaway,
a beautiful stallion, is threatened. Can
Nicky lay a vengeful past to rest – before
something terrible happens?

Another book in the Shock Shop series . . .

Coming soon . . .

Hairy Bill

Susan Price

Something came down the chimney in Alex's
bedroom in the night – something that
paused and, in a Scottish accent, asked for
Mathesons. Alex thought he was dreaming.
But his mum's name is Matheson. And when
he goes downstairs the next morning,
something is clearly very wrong.

The house is unnaturally, indeed
frighteningly, tidy. Has there been a break-in
– by obsessively tidy thieves? Or is there
another, more sinister explanation? Meet
Hairy Bill – a Scottish supernatural
whirlwind of terrifying tidiness.